T0370523

LOVE TRIANGLE

Shane Mealue
and
Monique Mealue

Order this book online at www.trafford.com
or email orders@trafford.com

Most Trafford titles are also available at major online book retailers.

Printed in the United States of America.

ISBN: 978-1-4669-3393-4 (sc)
ISBN: 978-1-4669-3394-1 (e)

Trafford rev. 05/07/2012

 www.trafford.com

North America & international
toll-free: 1 888 232 4444 (USA & Canada)
phone: 250 383 6864 ♦ fax: 812 355 4082

Other books by Monique Mealue and *Shane Mealue

Johnny's first job
Johnny goes shopping
Camping trip you will never forget
*Personal vendetta
Short stories you will never forget
*Overcome the hands that's dealt
*Swift Justice
Adventure of life

I want to thank God, my husband who co-wrote this book and my son Ray who supported me in writing this book.

About the Author

I live with my husband for fourteen years and Ray in McMinnville, Oregon.

Prologue

Julie Guthrie is an attractive fair skinned reporter for the channel two news that is broadcasted from Santa Monica California. She has been with the local television station for seven years enjoying her career in front of the camera. The single woman with shoulder length straight red hair has a cute female Boston terrier name Muffy.

Staying healthy by exercising is a regular routine in the TV personality's weekly schedule as well as watching her diet for the most part.

Dates over the years have been few and far between from the independent woman focusing on her career not really giving a whole lot of thought about the opposite sex.

After several years of hit and miss dating, Julie becomes close to two very different kinds of men almost at the same time.

The first guy she meets is a clean cut well-dressed lawyer name Mark Hansen and the other is a thick bearded long haired commercial welder.

Both of the fellas enjoy doing the same things as she does which enrich the news reporter's existence in her Southern California home town.

Everything starts out light and fun before the complications ensue for Guthrie in the three way love triangle that was never expected to start.

In succession to seeing the two men for a few months, the broadcaster finds out she is pregnant. The careless young woman has no idea which of them is the responsible party that did the deed.

Chapter 1

Julie Guthrie a thirty two year old woman is working out at one thirty four Monday June twenty ninth 2011 at Better Fit Gym in Santa Monica California. She is a fair skin pretty young lady with a slender build standing at five foot six inches tall.

Ms. Guthrie has green eyes and red straight shoulder length hair that is in a ponytail, who is dressed in a red tank top with back Capri pants.

Tammy Nelson is a toned athletic built thirty three year old woman that is five-six tall that is peddling beside her best friend Julie since high school. Mrs. Nelson is dressed in a loose fitting hot pink V-neck cotton T-shirt with cotton blue running shorts.

The pair meets at least twice a week to sweat it out using stationary bikes, stair climbing machines and light free weight workout.

They have members since the large local gym opened four years earlier in their hometown. Both women joined as members after the free thirty day trial was over.

On the wall is a thirty two inch LED TV set that is displaying a professional golf game at California's beautiful Pebble beach Golf course.

"What are you going to do for the fourth of July weekend Julie?" Tammy asked looking over to her friend.

"I'm debating about going to the party that the Spark Broadcast Network is throwing at the Harrison Hotel in Malibu Beach." Guthrie replies while breathing hard.

"If you can't decide why don't you come to the "Oasis", my husband and I are having a seventies-eighties music band that will be playing at the lounge."

Both of them climb off their stationary bicycles snatching small white towels that are close by them. Each woman starts wiping the perspiration from their face and necks.

They have finished their rigorous two hour exercise routine for the day as they walk toward the woman's locker room, "Your invitation is certainty tempting but I'm going to need a little time to think over Tammy!"

"There is going to be a lot of hot guys at my business dancing and having a good time!"

"I don't know why you own a bar when you don't even drink alcohol?"

"The booze that I don't drink is more money in my pocket from the folks who do. Heck Brian drinks enough for the both of us!"

Following taking hot showers, the two friends have lunch at the Cedars Mill Café across the street from their twenty four hour gym.

Each of them is having something different for their late lunch together. Julie is eating the six inch wheat sandwich with fries while Tammy just has a bow of salad because recently put on a few pounds in the mid-section.

On the wall are old black and white framed pictures from movies that starred James Dean, Marylyn Monroe, Humphrey Bogart just to name a few.

Before going to her apartment Julie goes to her elderly neighbors carrying her blue nylon duffle bag by the black handles in her small left hand.

Jimmy and Carol Sharpton in apartment fifteen two doors from where she lives have been watching her little dog name "Muffy" that is two and a half years old.

She is a black and white pure bred Boston terrier with dark brown bulgy eyes to go with the bunny rabbit like ears that stick straight up.

Mr. and Mrs. Sharpton have been babysitting the pooch for almost as long as the small canine has been alive for twenty dollars a week.

They truly enjoy having "Muffy" around; the money is just a sweet added perk for them. Julie provides dog food along with various treats she gets from the grocery store.

Ms. Guthrie visits the old married couple drinking a can of lemon lime soda that was offered to her as she listens to the Sharpton's stories from the past.

She is seated on a light brown vinyl recliner holding "Muffy" in her lap in the pair's small living room. A twenty seven inch color tube television is playing a soap opera with the volume turned low. None of them are paying attention to the television while they enjoy each other's company.

An hour later, Julie leaves Jimmy and Carol's cozy one bedroom flat to go to her own small dwelling a short distance away.

In her two bedroom apartment, Ms. Guthrie puts Muffy down on the living carpet, so she can gather up her dirty clothes to the small washer in far side of the bathroom. While the clothes are washing, Julie takes the energetic terrier out her front door on a leash.

She tries to walk her young dog at least once a day for an hour for Muffy's well-being. Briskly they perambulate on the sidewalk to the big city park two blocks away from the apartment complex.

It feels good to have the warm sunshine on her face strolling along on the double wide grey concrete path in Whitmore City Park.

Guthrie pleasantly smiles then says, "Hello" to the other pedestrians that come her way previous to passing as they travel in other direction.

Some are walking their pets or their baby strollers casually enjoying the scenic site with trees and picnic areas. The content Boston terrier seems to smile as she pants while her short legs quickly moves along on the cement.

Back at the apartments, Julie drops her lovable pooch off once again with the caring Sharptons so she can quickly put a load of clothes in the dryer.

Julie has a short amount of time before she has to be at KZTV's broadcast station building across town for the channel two's six o clock news.

Her job is to report local as well as national headlining stories on camera in the modest size studio with twenty eight year old Kristy Monroe who does the weather.

Sometimes Ms. Guthrie has to take her turn at playing the role of a field reporter at the site of an event whether it is good or bad time to time.

Having an upbeat attitude, the attractive TV personality is listening to a country cd while driving her dark green 2010 Toyota Camry four door Sedan to work.

It is her normal route to the station she is taking on the sunny summer day to the TV station she's worked at for almost six years now.

Reaching the security guard's gate at the entrance of the Broadcast studio, Julie stops her compact foreign car beside the window of the small booth.

The stocky Mexican guard name Manuel slides open the glass to investigate who it is, "Good afternoon Ms. Guthrie. How you doing today?"

"Very well Manuel. How about yourself?"

"Same ole same ole being the keeper of the gate," He presses a button to lifting the long metal arm up allowing the female broadcaster to slowly pull forward.

She pulls into a spot that has a sign that reads "reserved for Julie Guthrie." Subsequent to grabbing her small leather satchel with important paper work inside, the journalist locked her driver side door.

Upon coming the building's dark grey metal door with the key pad entry lock just above the stainless steel handle the red headed woman pushes a five digit code. A metallic sound is made then followed by a green light indicating access.

Julie pulls up on the shiny metal level pushing the heavy door open promptly stepping inside the air conditioned east side portion of the news station.

Walking down the hall to her small cubicle Ms. Guthrie says, "Hi" to her fellow co-workers in a cheerful manner. Once inside the small cubicle that is bordered tan partitions she places the leather bag on the wood surface of her desk.

Carefully the news caster sits down upon the black fabric swivel chair unzipping the work bag pulling out paper containing stories.

Several sheets were faxed to her earlier in the day by KZTV's program director.

A focused correspondent intently reviews the typed out notes, when the station's manager Sherece Johnson walks up to Julie with a clipboard in her hand.

The African American woman who's in her late forties has been in charge of channel two's building almost ten years in the city of Santa Monica. She is a light complected skin, heavy set lady that's on a strict diet because of her diabetes.

"Ahem, excuse me, sorry to bother you! I have attendance list for the networks corporate Fourth of July party. Have you decided yet, I need to turn it in by tomorrow afternoon?"

"Oh, I'm not sure I want to go."

In succession to explaining in detail all the festivities that are going to occur thanks to the networks owner Theodore Andrew Sparks.

News broadcaster Guthrie signs the list then Mrs. Johnson briefly thanks her before continuing onto the next subordinate employee's cubicle.

Promptly she returns to studying the evening stories to ready herself for the verbal presentation that will be displayed on thousands of television screens.

"Attention everyone, we are going live in a half an hour! Please be ready ladies and gentleman!" Producer Jonathon Kozerski announces over the intercom system.

Julie has already quietly rehearsed reading out loud what is to be her evening news monologue to the viewers. She grabs her notes off her cluttered desk prior to the broadcast news set that is northwest portion of the cinderblock building.

The long legged reporter briskly strolls down the hall making her to the room where all the magic happens. Her high heels are making a clicking sound on the glossy white tile floors hard surface.

Upon striding down a long hallway Ms. Guthrie makes a left toward the good size studio room. Firmly she pushes one of the stainless steel bars of the beige metal double doors.

Inside there are the usual behind news crew's members hustling about readying the equipment for the late afternoon telecast.

A careful young journalist keeps a close eye on the ground as she steps over various cables and power cords that are strung out.

In the short distance ahead Julie sees usual well lighted set stage with a high wide counter that she sits behind on a tall padded stool.

Guthrie is walking to the left of the large boxy black camera one that is attached to a sturdy metal tripod to get to the stage's three steps.

"Hey is that a new outfit you are wearing today?" Bob Crandall who operates the first camera inquired about the lavender blouse, matching colored high heels and the knee length blue skirt.

She stops and turns facing the gentleman who's in his early fifties with a beer belly that is slightly hangs over his belt buckle.

The salt and peppered haired man with the thick overgrown mustache that covers his upper lip almost always has something to say to the pretty news caster.

Looking down at her attire, Guthrie says, "This old thing, I've had these threads for years just don't wear it often."

"Wish I could keep my clothes looking new, anyway good luck up there tonight young lady."

"Thank you Bob!"

Julie takes the short of steps on the left side of the stage to go take a seat at her usual position on the news set. She is prepped by her makeup artists shortly after sitting down on the tall stool.

While having a little touch up done to her face the journalist views Tim Dennison the lighting technician adjusting lights that are facing her.

Two other camera operators on Bob's right side finish up readying their large pieces of equipment prior to the telecast that is to start in fifteen minutes.

"I heard you're going to the Fourth of July party?" Kristine Monroe the weather forecaster walks up standing beside her as the sound man clips on a tiny mic onto the shirt of the evening news anchorwoman.

"Yes I am how did you know!"

"I asked Sherece if you signed on to go. Do you know what you are going to wear?" The twenty eight year old young lady with the short styled brunette asked.

"Right now Kristine I have no idea!"

"Ladies we're on in five minutes!" The second cameraman said after hearing Jonathon from his ear piece.

Set director Anthony Fontana rolls up the teleprompter between camera one and two turning on the twenty inch screen for Julie to read off of.

That evening Ms. Guthrie covers her usual local stories that had occurred in the Santa Monica community. For the most part the bad events outweighed the good as she spoke about recent criminal activities.

The attractive news reporter told a few national stories in the country following Kristine's weather report. Monroe talked about the summer heat wave that is forth coming in the month of July.

That night driving home she thinks to herself "What am I going to wear to the event. I need to have something on that's going to catch a hot guy's attention. Hopefully I'm going to meet someone there; I haven't dated very much in three years now!"

Walking to her apartment at eleven thirty in the evening, Julie as usual leaves Muffy overnight at the Sharpton's place until morning.

Chapter 2

The next morning at ten Julie is rummaging through her bedroom closet subsequent bringing her Boston terrier home from the elderly's couple apartment. Muffy is staring at her owner while lying on the full size bed with its head resting on her little paws.

She systematically slides hangers each with an article of clothing on them quickly from left to right. "I have nothing to wear and definitely I need to go shopping at "Gabrielle's fashion Boutique," even though there are a lot apparel hanging up and one long row of shoes on the closet floor.

"You're coming shopping with me, my sweet little muffin! You want to go, don't cha! Don't cha!" Guthrie enthusiastically says to her dog causing the small pooch to stand to its small feet.

Picking up Muffy then grabbing her purse off the night stand next to the bed's headboard walking toward the front door, when the phone begins to ring.

Putting the dog down on the dark grey medium shag living room carpet to answer the phone mounted on the wall in the dining room.

"Hello?"

"Is there a Ms. Guthrie there?"

"Yes, this is her speaking. How may I help you?"

"My name is Carrie Brightwood from the court house helping with jury duty. You forgot to show up on Monday for pre-selection of jurors."

"Oh that's right! I totally forgot about that. Is there a way I can make it up?"

"Tomorrow at eight is the deadline to make it up Ms. Guthrie."

"I'll make it a point to be there tomorrow Mrs. Brightwood!"

Instantly Julie calls up Sherece asking for a couple of days off regarding jury duty.

Mrs. Johnson has no problem letting her main evening news anchor have two days off. She has field reporter Abbey Hernandez fill in as usual when an employee cannot be at work.

Driving on Santa Monica Blvd where Ms. Guthrie goes shopping for her favorite apparel pondering about what kind of outfit she wants to purchase.

At the shop, Julie pushes open the glass door with the small brass bell tied to the inside handle making it rings as she comes in.

The shopaholic has her little black and white snuggly cradled in her right arm when the owner strolls toward her from helping a customer.

Gabrielle Badeau is a short petite French woman in her mid-fifties that still looks like she's in her early forties with black bobbed hair with a little grey in it.

She has owned the business for a little over twenty years at the same location with great success with her husband who passed away a few years earlier.

"Welcome back dear! You brought my favorite bunny eared girl with you!" Gabrielle said as she petted Muffy's soft short fur on her head. "What can I help you with today?" Mrs. Badeau inquires with a strong French accent.

"I'm looking for something for a fourth of July party as well as another outfit for jury duty!"

"We got a few new outfits today. Would you like to see them?"

"Of course I do! You know how I am!"

"Yes I certainly do!"

The French woman takes her eager customer to her designated new arrival rack where they are hanging. While holding up a dress for Ms. Guthrie to observe the bell chimes indicating someone has entered the store.

"Please excuse me for a moment my dear." Badeau says before walking away to help a pair of older woman who have come in.

Placing the pooch down, Julie gives the clothing a good look over for thirty minutes holding each item close to her body.

She finds three suitable garments of clothing that will fit her size four frame that beautifully made. Two outfits are for the Fourth of July company event.

Her picks are a Seamless Rib blue tank top with a skirt with a Batik pattern that goes down to her knees. The other article is a red two piece Miraclessuit Norma Jean swim suit.

For the more business like attire Guthrie chose the baby blue Foxcroft stretch poplin shirt with black cotton pants. The news caster didn't want the style to revealing or to formal; luckily the garments are a balance between the two.

That night lying in bed with her dog, she is worried that the wrong person will be convicted or will be set free by her decision. Julie has never been selected for jury duty before and really has no idea what is expected of her.

Whimpering awakens the single woman from her slumber as she lies on her dozing. Muffy's mouth is close to her owner's right ear notifying that she needs to be taken out to use the restroom.

"Alright! Alright I'm getting up!" Julie declares looking at the impatient little dog through red tired eyes.

Upon coming back inside her home, Guthrie can't help but play around with her lovable pooch, who's a bit hyper following doing her business.

Promptly by seven-thirty, the potential juror is pulling out of the apartment complex parking lot with her small purse on the passenger seat.

She has one her favorite country cd's softly playing in the Camry's deck while making her way for the four mile trip to the large court house building.

Tuesday morning is another beautiful sunny day in her California town with the forecast predicted to be in the mid-eighties all week. There are plenty of commuters sharing the road with the local television personality.

In succession to parking her compact vehicle on the third level of the parking garage, Julie takes the elevator to the ground floor.

Inside the entrance of the ten story justice center, the nervous young lady strides up the steep set of marble stairs to the security booth.

A middle age man in a dark blue uniform comes out of the office asking, "May I help you mam?"

"I've been scheduled to come today for jury duty and I forgot to ask what room it is in."

"It is located in room 422 on the fourth floor. You can use the elevator by the stairs." He says pointing to his right.

"Thank you very much!" Julie replies with pleasant smile before walking away.

On the fourth floor there are many doors on both sides of the wide hallway as she slowly strolls along reading plaques searching for room 422.

At the end of the hall is a woman in her late forties sitting behind a wooden desk with a piece paper attached to a brown clipboard.

Ms. Guthrie steps in front of the slightly overweight Caucasian woman wearing big transparent plastic framed glasses.

"I'm Julie Guthrie, here for Juror's selection."

The lady looks down at her list using her index finger to scroll down the names that are typed on the white sheet of paper.

"Ah, here you are!" A formal sounding volunteer said as she marked off the name using a yellow highlighter pen, "You may go in; there are various drinks in the refrigerator along with hot beverages."

Inside the large room of 422, the green eyed woman dressed in the casual suit is handed a large folder of different forms to fill out.

She sees a long row of black padded chairs with metal legs on both sides of the room at the far end of spacious room is a long metal table.

Opening the folder, Julie sees a small blue paper with bold black print stating juror number #47. Going through the packet of paperwork the young lady fills out each form writing down personal information.

There are at least seventy people present, some are standing while others are seated about. Julie notices an empty seat by at table she chooses to sit at to fill out the forms.

Shortly before eight thirty, the woman in the hall comes into the room through the tall dark stained wooden door. She strolls to the left placing the clipboard onto the white counter surface that's before the row of chairs.

"Ladies and gentleman may I have your attention! Welcome to jury selection. My name is Marie Sanchez, I will be going over the several forms you all have been given. Followed by that you'll be viewing a twenty minute video on our new forty two inch flat screen TV's." The woman with the short black feminine style hair wearing a form fitting navy blue skirt speaks up to the attentive audience.

Julie glances to the big screen television's that are mounted on the walls to the left of her and the other is behind to the right of where she is sitting.

Speaking clear as well as to the point the volunteer goes over each form in detail while the people are seated with their paperwork.

Upon finishing she swiftly perambulates to the DVD player in a small office turning on the informative disc about jury duty.

Just as soon as the video was over, a bald man with a thick brown mustache wearing long black robe and red tie makes his presence known.

"Thank you everyone for taking time out of your busy lives to be here! We will be selecting several people on two separate cases that are to be tried within our court rooms by randomly choosing your juror number. Some of you will be picked by the attorneys; others will be set free to carry out your lives in the community." Judge Roy Miller said in his baritone voice.

Soon after the average built justice of the peace spoke, he chose thirty two individuals from the list he has in his left hand in front of him. One behind the other the men and women are led into a court room close to the elevator.

"For you remaining here before me, if I call your number please walk down the hall to court room 434 where you will be evaluated as a potential candidate." Sanchez states after adjusting her bulky eye glasses on her face.

Quite a few numbers were called out before the news reporter heard 47 crisply spoken from the lips of Marie. She gets up from the padded seat, taking her necessary items to the next stage of events down the hallway.

Coming into the courtroom, there is an isle that separates the eight rows of wooden backed bench seats. There are twenty of the chosen jurors seated on the first on the first two rows as the green eyed red head makes her way on the short red carpet in the room.

She sits in the front row next to a mid-twenty year old Mexican woman with long black waist long hair that is in a single braid running down her back.

To the front of everyone at two separate tables is the female prosecuting attorney on the left seated looking at her notes on the table.

Sitting with his client is a male attorney whose head is turned as speaks with the man in his late forties wearing an orange jail jumpsuit.

The whole room gets to their feet when the dark skinned black judge makes it up to his bench front and center. Upon telling everybody to be seated, the educated court leader explains the case at hand.

Judge Larry Myers has a deep voice that keeps the men and woman before him at attention to what he is explaining with authority.

A short time later, Ms. Guthrie along with eleven other people was politely asked to be seated in the juror box on the right side of the room.

One person at a time was asked a specific question their thoughts about the charges by the two well-groomed lawyers that speak eloquently.

After every candidate was questioned, the justice of the peace has the pair of attorneys met with him in his chambers to the rear of his stand.

Thirty minutes later the three of them came strolling out back to their seats. The clean shaven man sitting up higher than everybody else with the wooden gavel resting before him called out numbers.

Intently the local news caster listens for her number as she stares up the judge who is reading off a list on a white sheet of paper.

"It would be kind of cool to participate in the decisions that could change a person's life. On the other hand I do have other things to do in my daily schedule." Julie thinks to herself while listening.

When the last number is called, she didn't hear her number and the judge said, "For those of you that didn't hear your assigned number, you are dismissed from jury duty."

Chapter 3

Leaving the medium size room the former juror is sort of disappointed that she wasn't picked for the trial. Guthrie thinks to herself, "Heck, I would have probably found him guilty anyway. People who deal with drugs are always guilty in my heart."

A health conscience young woman walks past the sets of elevators deciding to take the staircase down on the left. Her brown leather dress shoes click as she briskly shuffles down the finished concrete steps.

Looking down at her feet while moving along the red head with shoulder length hair is suddenly bumps into a solidly built man.

She peers up with her bright green eyes viewing a slightly tanned blue eyed handsome man with short blond hair that is combed to the right.

"I'm so sorry; I was hustling up the steps not paying enough attention to where I was going! I sincerely hope that you are alright Miss!"

"I am fine sir! It was just as my fault that we ran into each other as it was yours."

"Hope you have a pleasant afternoon." The attractive man wearing an expensive looking dark grey suit says before flashing a glossy white smile.

"You too," Julie says smiling back at him just prior to making her past him.

"Boy what a good looking guy! A man like that is probably happily married with a few kids." Ms. Guthrie's mind ponders as she continues down the stairway to the main floor.

The loud sound of footsteps quickly approaching behind her fills the journalist's ears. She instinctively stops then turns to see who it is.

"As I was going up the steps I started realizing I've seen you someplace before. I'm probably wrong on this, but aren't you Julie Guthrie from the channel two news?"

"Yes I am. You happened to be the first person I have come into contact with today that recognized me." Shyly the TV personality responds softly.

"I usually don't do this so please don't be creeped out! Can I offer you a cup of coffee to get to know you sometime?"

"By the way, what is your name?"

"Excuse my bad manners! My name is Mark Hansen; I'm an attorney at law for the firm of Hansen and Ramel here in the city."

"I don't know Mr. Hansen!" Julie responds looking up playing hard to get with a man she feels attracted to.

The thirty five year old lawyer with the athletic frame prods her a bit more. He convinces the pretty young red head to join him at The Fresh Start cafe across the street from the court house.

"Ok, when did you have in mind to have this take place together?"

Looking at his flashy gold wrist watch, "It is close to three, I can meet you after I pick up a client's folder upstairs within twenty minutes time if that's alright?"

"Right now I don't have any prior engagements this afternoon so I don't mind waiting a bit. While I'm there I can get a bite to eat I'm pretty hungry right now."

"I'll hurry as fast as I can Ms. Guthrie, be there shortly!" He told her while scurrying up the stairs.

In the coffee shop, Julie perambulates up to the enclosed glass counter that has several different sandwiches, pasta dishes along with cold dessert plates.

At the cash register a bubbly teenager with her long brown hair pulled back into a ponytail greets the hungry patron cheerfully, "Hi, is there something that I can get for you?"

"I would like a ham and turkey on rye sandwich along with a medium mocha java please.

"That will be ten dollars fifty seven cents with tax included mam!" The young journalist pays with a twenty dollar bill she takes from her black leather purse.

After promptly handing over the change from the cash register the cashier politely says, "Please have a seat and I will bring it to you."

Glancing around Guthrie observes several people scattered throughout the room some are seated talking to each other and others are focused their laptop computers.

She finds a two person booth deep in the café in the right hand corner. It is a cozy semi private spot that is in the close proximity to the restrooms.

Julie sits down facing the entrance so she can see when Mark comes through single glass door. In a matter of minutes the slender employee of the business wearing an orange summer dress sets down Ms. Guthrie's order.

As she takes bites from her thick sandwich, the news reporter sees two women sitting across from each other by the front window. They are chatting back and forth sipping once in a while from their white cups.

Holding up her left wrist noticing it is three seventeen in the afternoon according to the tiny hands on her petite woman's watch.

Only seventeen minutes have elapsed since Julie came into the nearby establishment but for some reason it seems much longer.

"Am I really doing the right thing meeting some strange fella that I just met at the Santa Monica justice center building a few minutes ago?" The anxious woman mouths to herself after swallowing a bite of food.

Taking a last large bite of the delicious deli sandwich, the tall handsome lawyer briskly enters the coffee shop with a briefcase down at his side.

"Excuse me for running a little late; I had to go over a few briefs with my assistant that is struggling with some legality issues in our case."

Julie can only nod in understanding with her mouth full of food, as she tries to chew up the meaty mess up as fast as she can.

Guthrie hand gestures for the sharp dressed gentleman to have a seat on the opposite side of her as she swallows down her food.

Upon placing his dark burgundy leather briefcase down on the red vinyl cushioned booth seat scooting it over, Mark Hansen leisurely sits down.

Channel two's lead evening news anchorwoman softly giggles from reflecting back to her earlier awkward moment. "I was beginning to think you stood me up and I was about to leave in five minutes mister if you didn't get here." She jokingly said trying not smile.

"Believe me not making it here would be the last thing that I would want to do today! I'm glad you stuck it out to talk to me Ms. Guthrie."

"Please call me Julie; I don't like formality very much Mr. Hansen!"

"Call me Mark if you would!" He says while chuckling.

"Do you mind if I grab another cup of mocha?" She asked looking into his blue eyes.

"Sounds like a good idea, I think I will join you I love their delicious blends of coffee."

Following the well-spoken legal professional paying for both of their hot beverages, the pair made themselves comfortable again at the booth.

"I have watched your news cast for a little over two years now and can hardly believe that I'm seated across from you at a coffee shop!"

"Thank you very much; I am flattered you feel that way about me!"

"How long have you been a news caster?"

"I started working on air at public broadcast channel for very little money, was employed there for close to three years before going to KZTV. That means I've been with channel two now for seven years."

"How do you like being in front of the camera for thousands of viewers to watch?"

"For me I have always been a ham in front of any kind of camera, even when I was just a little girl growing up. What kind of job do you have that you wear a fancy designer suit like you have on?"

"I am an attorney at law with the law firm of Hansen and Romel. Basically I'm a hired hand for the company that my older brother Carl started with his partner Brent Romel."

"Sounds like a meaningful occupation not to mention a well-paying one to boot! Your wife or girlfriend isn't going to walk in here and be mad that you're having coffee with me?"

"To answer the first part of the question, I have never been married but I broke up with a longtime girlfriend a couple of months ago. As attractive as you are, there will probably be a big muscle bound man storming in here angry about our get together."

"Mark I haven't had a serious relationship for almost four years! Not even a whole lot of dates because of focusing on being a dependable career woman."

"A pretty lady like yourself who speaks eloquently should absolutely have no trouble whatsoever landing a guy."

"Thank you for your generous compliment." She replies smiling flirtatious while brushing her hair back.

"I can't believe that our country's Independence Day is only a few days away." Hansen states prior to taking a sip from his luke-warm coffee.

"Speaking of the Fourth of July my company is having a party at the Harrison Hotel in Malibu, would you like to come?"

"I've stayed there a couple of time, it's a fancy place. Boy I'd love to come but I have a golf tournament that I'm playing in. Friday the third I don't have any set plans in the evening and I would love to take to an elegant dinner!"

"You'll have to let me think about it for a while." Julie teases him.

"It's my birthday that day and I desire to have the company of a charming woman such as yourself on my special day."

23

"Ok you twisted my arm! I'll be escorting you to dinner birthday boy!"

Before leaving the quaint coffee shop, they exchange addresses and phone numbers. Julie notices that Mark is driving a shiny silver 2011 Mercedes-Benz C-class Sedan.

Friday night at seven, Guthrie takes Muffy out for short walk to do her business outside. She decided to leave the adorable little Boston terrier at home since the date shouldn't take any longer than a couple of hours.

"Ding Dong, Ding Dong!" Sounds the doorbell ten minutes till eight that evening at the news personality's small suitable apartment.

An excited young woman hurries to her front door wearing an ankle length black dinner dress that she hasn't worn in quite some time.

Opening the white door, she sees the tall handsome attorney that's dressed in a dark blue dress shirt with a grey tie that matches his khaki pants.

Mark has a bouquet of red roses in his left hand and a bottle of 2002 Dom Perignon champagne in the other, "Mr. Hansen, it's supposed to be your birthday not mine. I'm the one that should be giving you a gift not the other ways around."

"My present is your pretty face glowing across the restaurant's table from me this warm summer evening in July." He says handing the expensive things to her awaiting feminine hands.

"Thank you so much for the rather spendy items. Please come in while I put these away! Make sure you shut the door, I don't Muffy to get out!"

"Who's Muffy Julie?" Guthrie's date asked as he shuts the front door, when two quick barks erupts a short distance from him. "Oh you must be Muffy!" Mark declares looking at the small black and white dog that is staring at him with curiosity in her bug eyes.

"I see you've met my lovable mutt." She says finding her date on his knees petting the short haired dog's fur.

"Yes, yes I have and she's quite a cutie pie! I have a male French bulldog who looks similar to this one named "Hugo." "Are you ready to go Mark?"

"Yes mam!" The well-dressed lawyer says getting to his feet accompanying her out of the cozy flat.

Luckily a large maroon SUV was pulling of a parking spot in front of the old red bricked Italian restaurant that has tables outside for patrons to eat at.

Quickly the attorney at law snags up the vacant spot pulling in close to the curb with his fine mid-size four door German automobile.

Inside the establishment they walked up to male host, who takes them to the table out in front of the building then hands them menus to peruse over.

Sitting down the red head sees two long stem wine glasses with cloth napkins neatly folded inside of them on top of the small table with the white table cloth on it.

When the waiter with the short cropped black hair and tightly groomed goatee came to the couple's table they have their minds made up.

"Good evening folks, are you ready to order now?" The olive skinned server inquires with a slight Italian accent.

"Yes, we'll both have the Tuscan grilled lamb chops with rice pilaf and steamed vegetables." Mark's tenor voice crisply said.

"Very good choice, would you like something to drink with your order tonight?"

"We each want a glass of Riesling white wine please." Julie chimes in informing the man that's jotting down the pair's request.

A few minutes later, a dark skinned young waitress brings two glasses of chilled white wine on a small circular black tray that she is holding with one hand.

The two take sips from their wine glasses in succession to showing the hospitable server appreciation before she leaves their table.

"Thank you so much for joining me on such a warm pleasant evening outside."

"Believe me, it is my pleasure to be here Mark. Besides I couldn't possibly leave you all by your lonesome on your birthday."

Acoustic music that is coming from the several small speakers that are mounted high on the building's veneer wall adds a pleasant atmosphere. It is low enough that you can easily hear it and for people to communicate with each other without having to shout.

"So what do you like to do for fun when you're hard at work in front of a television camera?"

"I like to go the gym to work up a good sweat; going for a long drive on a fairway isn't out of the question."

"You like to go golfing Julie!"

"I am a member at the White Wolf country club."

"Me too, we'll have to set up a tee time for just the two of us for a round of eighteen holes."

"You're on buster! I'm gunna see what your made of out there!" Mark lightly laughs after the comment from the pretty greened eyed girl.

The two casually talk back and forth after the hot meals were brought to them by the cheerful waiter with another basket of bread.

They each comment how good the food taste following taking bites from their shiny dinner forks.

Subsequent to finishing the last of her lamb another cold glass of wine is set down that she ordered a few minutes previously.

Being a responsible driver, Hansen declines having anymore alcohol so he may operate his Mercedes without being impaired whatsoever.

Ms. Guthrie is feeling a little buzzed following downing the last of the sweet tasting California Riesling. She places the empty stemmed glass down on the table in front of her slightly leaning forward on the table.

"Let me pay for at least half of the bill Mark." Julie says going in her purse that's on the slender woman's lap.

"You are my guest and I insist on paying every bit of the tab here tonight!" The good mannered gentlemen said looking at his date with sincerity showing in his blue eyes. Graciously she nods in approval knowing that the tan charmer was not going to be swayed into changing his mind.

After paying for the bill, the couple traveled back to Guthrie's apartment to mingle a little awhile to get to know each other more.

Inside the small pad, Julie turns on her compact stereo in the living room area. A free spirited woman decides to put on some romantic classic instrumental music to enhance her already euphoric mood.

The room is filled with the sounds of relaxing melodies that are composed by various well known composers. Julie persuades her sociable guest to have a glass of the expensive champagne that he brought over.

Both of them in a loose relaxed state of mind after a few drinks winding up slow dancing close together enjoy the feel of each other's body.

Hansen and Guthrie move graciously across the dark grey carpet in the direction of the news anchor's bedroom, when they started passionately kissing.

For a short time the pair slowly danced with each other while they blindly make out focusing on the intense heated moment ignoring everything around them.

Two impassioned people barely make it to the long black micro fiber couch before striping their clothes off. The athletic naked body of Hansen is on top of Guthrie's nude torso making love to her.

As the fulfilled red head is buttoning up her shirt, Muffy is by the front door circling around impatiently, "Please excuse me for a moment, I think someone over there needs a potty break outside!"

"Be my guest duty calls. Do you mind if I use your shower to freshen up Julie?"

"Have at it, just don't use up all the hot water because I'll be using it after you my good man!"

Outside walking the adorable black and white pooch, the attractive green eyed woman has a thought enter her mind, "It has been over a year since the last time I had sex before this wonderful night! I hope that he stays over."

A little before three in the morning, the news strolls up where the handsome is sitting on the couch playing with the affectionate Boston terrier. She has a white robe tied around her with a red bath towel wrapped around her head upon getting out of the shower.

Subsequently from looking at his watch, Mark observes that it is getting late then request to spend the night to Julie's delight.

Hansen's reason for his decision was that he felt a little intoxicated along with being tired.

Lying in bed, Julie puts her arm over the sleeping man's warm back prior to falling into a deep sleep with Muffy as usual at the foot of the full size bed.

While eating breakfast, the journalist sits down on the opposite of the small dining table placing her hot cup coffee down upon the surface.

"I don't know where you're at on what happened last night, but for me I'm not ready for a serious relationship to occur anytime soon."

"It was great love making last night between us! We are on the same page about taking it slow maybe even dating other people as we get to know each other!"

"You don't know how happy it makes me to hear that you have the same sentiment as I do!"

Chapter 4

Driving North on Pacific Coast Highway one along the ocean in her Toyota Camry heading to the Harrison Hotel that's close to the beach in Malibu. Julie has her medium size colorful beach bag filled with the new bathing suit along with sun tan lotion and other needed items.

It is a gorgeous sunny Saturday at two twenty one in the afternoon as she commutes with many other drivers on the busy freeway.

Peering through the windshield out in front of her, the TV personality is not paying attention to what is coming out of the car's speakers.

Just thinking about how much she liked being with the attractive lawyer along with other fun things they could do together down the road.

A smile crosses her glossy red lips as Julie sees a sign that reads Malibu five miles ahead in white reflective letters on a green road sign.

Passing a few bicyclists, Guthrie almost missed the left hand turn of the entrance to the Harrison Hotel. She slowly cruises into the shade of the covered front of the tall building.

The young lady views a couple of bell hops assisting guests with their luggage into the revolving door of the hotel along with well-dressed parking valets.

All of the hospitable employees are wearing short sleeves white dress shirts with dark blue ties, matching colored polyester vests and slacks.

Momentarily the news caster waits until the vehicle directly in front of her is moved so she can park next to the curb for assistance.

"Good afternoon miss! Would you like me to park your car for you?" A clean cut entrance attendant came to her driver's side door saying as soon as Julie stepped out of her four door compact Sedan.

She is wearing her recently purchased form fitting blue tank top, short matching skirt and comfortable pair of brown slip on sandals with short heels.

"Yes, you may!" The attractive woman with shiny shoulder length hair that's down said handing him her car keys before grabbing her bag from the passenger's side seat.

Following coming through the automatic glass revolving door with the beach bag over her shoulder, Julie observes several couches with paintings on the walls. It is a broad hallway where guests can wait for their automobiles in comfort.

Making an immediate left, Guthrie perambulates a short stretch then makes a right to the large main lobby to get to the front desk for information on where the parties held.

The fair skin green eyed woman can't help but look around the spacious room with the twenty foot high ceiling as she strolls to the other side.

There are spendy looking armchairs grouped together on top of gigantic Kasmar Persian rugs where many people are sitting with their luggage on their sides. Only a handful of children are present in the Harrison.

Prior to approaching the tall pink marble front counter that has two females and one male concierge helping folks, she views a large posted announcement.

On it is a directional arrow pointing right to where the, "Sparks Broadcast Network" is being held. "This is handy, now I don't have to ask one of the already front desk employees!" She softly says under her breath in front of the sign that is mounted on two vertical chrome metal poles.

Walking down the wide carpeted corridor, she begins to faintly hear music along with the sounds of people talking up ahead her on the left.

Almost at the end of the hallway, Julie notices two long set up folding tables spaced far apart from each other outside the convention rooms doors.

There are two women behind each of them checking off from a list then handing out name tags that will be placed onto individuals shirts.

The channel two news reporter steps up to the closest table to her, seeing Sherece Johnson seated on a metal folding chair looking up.

"Why are you out here instead of inside mingling about having fun boss?"

"You know how it is girl; I always have to keep a close watch on all of you!" Johnson replies than smiles big showing her white shiny teeth.

Guthrie was handed a white ping pong ball along with her sticker name tag. Looking down, "What in the world is this tiny ball for Sherece?"

"Here you go, use this to write your name on it. You're going to put this into the bingo tumbler by the deejay's stage. About every hour, the disc jockey is going to spin the round metal cage full of ping pong balls. He will three names each for various prizes from money, merchandize, trips and even and a couple of nights at this fine establishment." Mrs. Johnson informs Julie after handing a black permanent marker to write with.

Upon carefully writing her name on the small white ball's round surface she sticks the name tag that reads, "Julie" in big black letters onto her right side of her chest.

"Hope I see you inside later!"

"I'll be in there shortly to partake in the festivities Ms. Guthrie."

Inside the big banquet hall is a DJ wearing dark sun glasses, a loose fitting button up flowered Hawaiian shirt with long blue surfer shorts.

Straight ahead are network employees who are either seated at the provided tables or standing in gathered groups. They are chatting with each other while drinking cold beverages. Some are alcoholic drinks and some are non-alcoholic that the good size crowd are enjoying.

A small wet bar with a bartender is in right corner in the room that is the source of all the liquid refreshments. Next to the middle aged black man serving the drinks is the buffet that is being prepped by the catering service.

While casually strolling around the convention room, the news journalist briefly stops here and there chatting with fellow co-workers she knows.

Gazing at the ladies watch on her thin wrist, Julie realizes she has plenty of time to take a dip in the hotel's decent size outdoor swimming pool.

Briskly she strides outside to the pool house's changing area to put on her red two piece bathing suit. Upon leaving, Julie leaves her regular clothes in the beach bag she brought in the women's room.

A trim figured young lady walks barefooted to the aqua blue water of swimming pool that has a few people in the shallow end.

The warm sun shines down on her head as she perambulates passed men and woman under the large orange nylon umbrellas to the deep side of the pool. They are relaxing on their backs on white plastic lounge chairs.

Jumping feet first in the cool refreshing water, the fun loving beauty starts swimming laps for a work-out from one end to the other.

When three teenage boys show up and begin rough housing in the water, Guthrie says to herself "Looks like a good time to get out and catch some rays away from these jokesters!"

A cold slightly uncomfortable sensation comes over the slender body as Julie walks over to the complimentary white beach towels neatly folded on a cart.

Finding an empty long folding chair under the shade the young woman with the wet slick back hair lays the towel down on it.

Slowly the hotel guest lies down on her back to start taking it easy as a cool breeze comes across her wet skin. "I thought that was you swimming Julie!"

"Oh hi Kristine, how's it going?"

"Have you met my older brother Joe before?"

"No, no I don't think I have."

"This big bear of man beside me is Joe O'Connell. I want you to meet my co-worker Julie Guthrie."

"Nice to make your acquaintance," the six foot two stocky bearded man states prior to leaning down shaking her petite hand.

"Same here," the green eyed woman replied back.

The two of them started talking ignoring Kristine when she says, "I will leave you to alone while I find my husband Alex, he's probably going to try to drink all the free beer." Monroe says walking away to go inside.

Joe pulls up a chair from behind him scooting it close to where the woman in the red two piece bathing suit is on her back reclined.

"I've heard a lot of good things about you from little sister; she really enjoys working with you." O'Connell says as his kind brown eyes sincerely look into Julie's.

"I'm very glad that she feels that way. I share the same sentiment as she does."

"What do you do for a living?"

"I'm a union welder with the local 217. I am one of the people responsible for the structural welding on skyscrapers and bridges among other things here in California."

"Sounds like it keeps you busy," Guthrie says looking at the handsome man with the thick black bushy beard.

"My occupation most of the time leaves me with opportunities to go have a little fun! What do you enjoy doing besides swimming in hotel pools on nice sunny days?"

"Outdoor recreation brings me enjoyment in my life, helping me with unwanted stress."

"A good long road ride on my Harley Davidson road king calms my mood quite a bit."

"You have a motorcycle Joe? I haven't ridden on one since I was in my early twenties."

"It would be my pleasure to give you a ride on my bike somewhere sometime Julie."

"We'll have to get together and make that happen soon Joe." She tells showing her perfectly straight teeth while smiling at the tall man with the long black hair that's put in a ponytail.

While they were talking over the outside speakers, the wacky disc jockey announces, "The buffet is ready for all of you TV chicks and dudes to chow down at. I will be calling three more names for the drawing."

"Let's go inside for a bite to eat, I could use a beer anyhow!" He says looking down at her.

"You're on, first I need to go get changed!"

Like a true gentlemen, the burly man dressed in casual street clothes waits close to the pool house for Julie next to white painted block wall.

Strolling out, the fair skinned young lady notices a pleased look upon the rugged man's face once he sees her in the form fitting outfit.

Inside the banquet hall, Guthrie puts her beach bag next to the table that she will share with Joe, his sister and her husband Alex.

The hungry journalist loads her dinner plate with prime rib, baby red potatoes, and a creamy mushroom pasta dish with a warm butter roll.

Their table has friendly conversation while everyone partakes in the delicious hot food. A young server in her early twenties brings bottles of domestic beer as well as other cold drinks.

Joe and Julie definitely share a connection with each other as they are seated close to one another communicating and sharing a laugh once in a while.

"Right now is time for the final names to be called out by my glamorous self!" The hyper DJ shouts into the microphone quieting the roar of the crowd in front of him.

He starts turning the crank on the wheel rapidly spinning the many small white balls in a fast circular motion. "Tim Dennison's name is the first one is announced over the loud PA system."

Julie hollers out, "Way to go Timmy my man," as the slightly embarrassed long blonde hair lighting technician walks up to the stage.

The next person he called was Julie Guthrie's name who won a two night stay at the Harrison Hotel, "Who's going to be the lucky person that you take Julie?" Kristine asks looking across the table to her.

Not responding to the inquiry, she slyly grins at her teasing co-worker standing from the chair before going up to receive her prize.

Following the disc jockey putting on some pop rock music, people commence to bop about dancing with each other in the open area by the stage.

In the middle of changing a record from the turntable, the fun loving DJ notices off in a distance out of the window a large glow.

He looks at his digital watch realizing he has worked past his eight pm cut off time. "Guys and gals it looks like there is a bon fire raging out on the beach."

Everyone is slowing leaving with their cold drinks from the convention room as the hired entertainer packs up his equipment.

Guthrie and O'Connell wait until the crowd thins down before exiting toward the beach. "I really love a gigantic outdoor fire." Julie says strolling next to the big biker looking guy by the outdoor pool fence.

"Me too, it reminds me of camping in the woods roasting hot dogs." Joe adds just before taking a sip from his half full bottle of beer.

Nearing the tall bon fire they see four men and four women singing Hawaiian songs on the soft white sand. Two of the men are quickly strumming brown ukulele.

The pair stands close to each other as they watch the musicians standing and siting off to the side the bright fire that is putting out a great deal of heat.

Less than an hour lapses by, Joe glances over to Julie, "It's a beautiful night, do you want to go for a little stroll down the beach?"

"Big guy I thought you'd never ask!"

Walking down the sandy shoreline hand in hand, the couple is going along beside the small blue green waves that gently crashed down on the sand. Bright and big in the dark sky is the full moon that shines over the vast Pacific Ocean.

They stop facing the white cap waves that reflect the back porch lights of the beach front houses. Joe gracefully leans down gently placing his lips on hers.

She is very receptive to the attractive male with the pony tail that goes to the middle of his back. Gusts of wind managed to find their way under the green eyed woman's skirt that put her even more in the mood.

A turned on California girl puts her arm around Joe pulling him closer to her body as they make out heavy as the salt water runs over their feet.

Out of the corner of his eyes views a short span away a white and blue ten by ten changing pavilion. Seductively the tall man whispers in the much shorter woman's right ear speaking his mind.

O'Connell leads the willing young lady by the hand thirty yards southeast from the water to the dark secluded area that has little light around it.

Chapter 5

Opening her top dresser drawer to snatch out her favorite pink cotton nightgown, Julie noticed her plastic birth control wheel container on top. She looks down discovering two pills are still in there slots when they should be missing. "Oh, I'm such an idiot! I can't believe that I now forget to take them now that I'm having sex again!"

In the morning after taking her tiny pill to get back her preventive schedule, "Quit worrying what are the chances of me getting pregnant without any kind of protection anyhow! It's got to be one in a million chances to occur."

Loudly the telephone rings in the kitchen while the news reporter is pouring a cup of coffee. Answering the phone she says, "Hello?"

"Hey it's me Joe; it's such a nice day and was wondering if you would like to go for a ride on the back of my bike?"

"Where are we going to go?"

"I was thinking of taking you to the Outback animal refuge forty miles north of town to take a guided jeep tour."

"Yeah that would be great. I haven't been there for a while Joe."

"What time is it a good for me to come pick you up at your place?"

"Give me at least an hour to shower and eat breakfast."

"You got it, see you soon!"

A few minutes after eleven she hears a hard rapping at the front door, opening it Guthrie sees burly bearded O'Connell holding a motorcycle helmet in his left hand. Joe hands the glossy black half helmet that Julie is going to wear while grinning.

"Thank you! I will be there in a minute; I need to make sure that my dog has enough food and water before I leave."

"Cool, I'll be waiting in the complexes north parking area by my Harley."

Cruising east on San Vicentle Blvd on the back of the roaring Harley Davidson, the red head with her hair pulled back in a pony holds onto Joe's waist.

Julie briefly sees a male behind the steering wheel with a female in the passenger seat of the foreign silver Sedan. She barely sees the blonde driver as it passes in the opposite direction through the dark sunglasses over her eyes.

"That couldn't have been Mark, could it?" Guthrie says to herself doing a double take.

It is a pleasantly warm summer day as the TV personality enjoys the wind on her face on the scenic road ride to their destinations.

At the animal sanctuary the couple takes a two hour expedition in a topless off road vehicle on a well-traveled path.

They sit close together in the back seat as the guide points out the wild animals native to Africa that is roaming about the dessert like property.

The perimeter fenced habitat has small trees that provide shade for the various wild life to take comfort under from the hot sun.

Julie is so glad she came viewing all the beautiful wild life that is off in the near distance while taking pictured from the digital camera she brought.

At the end of the tour she gracefully thanks the guide wearing the worn appearing tan ball cap with matching colored shirt and cargo pants.

Previous to going home, Joe treats his guest to a good meal at a road side family restaurant. "I love to take you camping sometime." Joe asks from across the table.

"That would be terrific, just so you know for now I want us to be friends."

"I understand you don't want to be tied down yet to any one guy! I'm cool with that aspect."

Shortly before five that afternoon, O'Connell motors them into the apartment complex parking lot. After the large motorcycle is shut off, the slender woman carefully swings her leg over the seat.

She looks up thanking Joe for the wonderful outing prior to a quick hug and a kiss on his hairy check before making her way the small apartment.

Every other day, Julie talks to Mark on the phone before having to go to work at the TV station. Guthrie only spoke to Joe once since the last time she saw him on Sunday.

The following week, Hansen convinces the hard working journalist to come with him to the outdoor farmer's market for fresh produce.

That Saturday the pair is browsing from vegetable stand to vegetable stand when Julie bumps into Joe who is walking beside a short Mexican woman.

"What a surprise to see you here Joe!"

"I'm just here with my next door neighbor Maria to pick up a few things because her car is broke down." Joe says when Mark steps up next to Julie holding a small yellow onion in each hand.

"I can't decide if I want the bigger one or the smaller of the two." He comments just prior to noticing the much taller man wearing a blue tank top.

"I want you to meet Joe O'Connell; He is my co-worker's brother." She says gesturing to the bushy bearded guy. "This is Mark Hansen a friend of mine."

"It's nice to meet you!" The attorney at law wearing a yellow polo shirt said to Kristine's older brother.

"Same here Mark!"

Later that evening, eating dinner at Hansen's twenty two hundred square foot home. "This is really delicious, what you have cooked here tonight!"

"My mom was a culinary chef before retiring, she taught me how to prepare meals at home in the kitchen."

"Last Sunday I thought I saw you driving with a woman close to the Balsa wood country club."

"Her name is Tina, she is a just a friend that I took golfing that day. It was nothing serious or anything."

"I'm not being jealous; I was merely wondering if it was you that I spotted. Besides I have been seeing Joe that you were introduced to earlier."

"Is he a gentleman when he is with you?"

"Yes Joe is very much so!"

After dinner the two went to Mark's spacious living room and watched a new released science fiction movie on blue-ray.

Guthrie is impressed with how vivid is on the eighty two inch LED television set. Playing host the attorney makes a big bucket of popcorn for them to share along with two cold can of pop to wash down the dry treat.

Before dropping Julie off at her apartment he asked, "I just got a new sailboat and was wondering if you would like to go sailing on Sunday July twenty six?"

"Sounds like a fun plan, where were thinking of going?"

"My thirty six foot vessel is tied to the dock at the "Tides End" harbor. We could go out on the Pacific Ocean from where it is kept, maybe afterwards have lunch at the Lagoona Inn restaurant."

"I like what I'm hearing; can I meet you there at ten in the morning at the parking area?"

"Right now that sounds pretty durable for me."

"I will give you a jingle a couple of days before the trip." Guthrie tells him then gives him a quick kiss on the lips prior to stepping out of the passenger side door.

Monday mid-morning, the drowsy woman with the messy red hair makes her way to the refrigerator. She is going for the coffee mate to cloud up her black coffee.

Closing the fridge's white textured door Guthrie notices her small calendar that's held up by a magnet. Her green eyes notice the week of July twenty six to August first off from work.

Julie had scheduled those vacation days months earlier. "I wonder if Joe's offer still stands for the camping trip somewhere." She thinks to herself reflecting back on what the scruffy handsome man said.

Strolling to the phone Guthrie calls up O'Connell's cell phone that he always keeps on hip unexpectedly, "I have a few days off and was wondering if you still want to go outdoor excursion?"

"What days do you have in mind?" She tells him, "Those days will be perfect, we will be finished with this project then I will have a little more than a week off before the next one." The Journeyman welder explains sitting with his co-workers on break.

"I will talk to you later Joe!"

"See you soon!"

That work week, the channel two broadcaster's mind was full of thoughts of the two trips that will occur so close together.

Julie field reported three out of the five days that was televised for viewers at home. A couple of news worthy stories was about violent criminals hurting people for money.

It gave her comfort to know that she was going to be out of the city having a good time relaxing away from the hustle and bustle.

Sunday at the "Tides End" half full parking area, the anxious young lady waits in her car with Muffy seated in the passenger seat.

She managed to find a spot facing the long wooden dock that has different size sailboats from one end all the way to the other. There is at least a hundred yards in length of tied up vessels with tall sails that stick up in the air.

Guthrie hears a couple of honks behind her, looking back she sees Mark's Silver Mercedes-Benz Sedan. He is backing the expensive vehicle on the driver's side of Julie's Toyota Camry.

She gets out with her small black and white pooch quickly attaching red nylon leash to the panting dog's collar. Hansen is carrying two tall transparent plastic water bottles when he approaches the fair skin woman in a tank top and shorts.

Mark and Julie are walking side by side down the wooden plank ramp with the dog in the lead toward the dock. It is a cloudy day but the sun is breaking through in the sky.

They make a right at the bottom of the steep entrance way then begin striding past the white bows of the tied up sailboats.

Flying seagulls are squawking around them as the couple briskly strolls on the wood surface that is gently bobbing up and down from the ocean. Muffy looks with curiosity around as her short legs steadily move.

The clean cut lawyer stops them in front of the thirty six foot floating vessel that is lightly swaying to and fro. It is a gorgeous white craft with two navy blue bands that wrap completely around the body.

"This is "Lady of the sea," let me hop up first so I can help you and Muffy on board."

"Did you come up with the name or one of your girlfriends?"

"That beautiful title is from yours truly! Not to mention you are the first woman that I've shown this to." He said right before getting on his sailboat.

"Here hand me the big eared beast first then I will give you a hand up next."

Upon coming aboard Julie sees that the fancy craft has a cozy interior cabin with padded bench seats. She gives her date plenty of room to hoist up the royal blue main sail.

Showing great efficiency the experienced sailor has the sleek vessel traveling west toward the open ocean. The bright warm sun is high in the sky after the clouds disperse in different directions.

A couple hours of mildly chopping waves on the vast body of deep salt water, Julie views the top of the grey whale.

Suddenly a powerful blast of water comes from the blow hole of the barnacle covered gigantic marine mammal. Another one quickly comes out of the water then splashes back down submerging itself under the water close to the first whale.

Mark's sailboat bobs up and down a lot higher from the wake the second huge sea creature created a short span from them. It made Muffy stagger about upon the tan deck as she wandered about.

"Wow! Did you see that Mark? My first experience seeing those massive things of beauty!"

"I've seen them quite a few times but not very often this close. I never get tired of sight of these gentle sea dwelling animals."

Time seems to fly by as the two shared wonderful moments with the cool ocean breeze on their skin. They are communicating while watching other sailboats off in the distance aimlessly floating on the choppy salt water.

Back in the parking lot after a late lunch, "Thank you so much for my first sailing trip in quite some time. I had a wonderful time with you and I look forward to spending more time with you Mark."

"It was my absolute pleasure to have you accompany me with your well behaved dog out on the big blue sea. When can I call you again?"

"I'm going to be out of town for a couple of days but I promise to call you as soon as I get back!"

Eight that evening Julie packs two big red duffle bags of her personal items and necessary things for Muffy. She even loads some canned foods in the mix before placing them by the front door.

All night lying in bed Guthrie is wondering about the camping trip. Her thoughts are on what will happen and what exciting thing she will do or see with her fellow vacationer.

Around nine thirty seven in the morning, O'Connell rings his female companion's doorbell when she was just putting the terrier in her little pink travel carrier.

Opening the white wooden door, "Great timing, I'm all packed up ready to go."

"Good deal pretty lady! Let me give you a hand with your things."

The big man helps the anchor woman by carrying both bags while she handles transporting Muffy to the parking area.

Joe places Julie's stuff in the almost completely loaded bed of his full size Ford extra cab pickup truck. His rig has camping gear, bundles of dry wood and a couple of fishing poles.

Making sure everything is tied down; the husky welder goes driver's side while Guthrie puts her dog behind the passenger's bucket seat on the floor.

Before driving off, O'Connell puts on the air conditioner rolling up both windows to keep everyone cool from the already fairly warm temperature.

On the way to the camp spot, the red head with the pony tail looks over from the passenger seat. "On the phone you didn't tell me very much. So where exactly are we going to stay at?"

"It's a surprise I know you will love!" He said still looking up ahead through the windshield.

Close to two hours later they are driving up to a booth where a woman in a state park uniform taking money at an open window.

She is dressed in a light brown button up long sleeve shirt with a large state patch on the right shoulder and a smaller one above her left front pocket.

The park ranger also has a dark brown pant that matches the cap with a patch on the front, "Welcome to Stillwater State park! Are you here for a day or overnight stay?"

"We're here going to be camping over for three nights."

"Do you have reservation here sir?"

"Yes I have!" Joe removes a piece of paper from the glove compartment, presenting it to the thirty something park employee.

"You go pass the bridge to where the camping area is located and here is the map to where your site will be." She says circling where it is on the black and white printed park map then hands it to him.

Slowly cruising on the two car wide black asphalt road on the right side Julie sees a big picnic area. Several people are playing disk golf on the spread out grassy course.

While others are eating outside on brown picnic tables with several people or riding their bicycles on one of the many bike paths.

"Certainly appears to be plenty to do here! I would love to try my hand at throwing Frisbees like they are."

"Don't worry you'll get your chance after we are done unpacking. I brought a few with me."

Going over the bridge, O'Connell passes a few tent sites before stopping at their space that has several trees surrounding it. The cozy camp area has a little stream behind it and short distance away is the bathrooms with showers.

Before backing up, Guthrie gets out of the vehicle to guide Joe back into the gravel parking spot as he looks in his side mirror.

Once the engine is shut off, the first thing that is removed from the six foot bed of the truck is the two rolled up bundles that make up the tent.

It took them almost a half an hour to fully set up the three person nylon shelter as they struggle to work together on the small project.

The second item was taken out was the queen size inflatable mattress that the pair took turns using the hand pumper.

After putting away most of the items into the tent, Joe grabs a small black duffle bag with a few plastic discs zipped inside.

"Let's get started before it gets late." A grinning burley guy declares slinging the strap over his shoulder.

The three of them strolled on the walking path in the sunshine to the starting point of the first hole. "This is a wonderful surprise; I have never been here before."

Following an hour of playing disc golf, the couple is strolling back to the camp site, "That was a lot of fun; I'm going to have to invest in a set of those plastic discs!"

"As well as you did on the course, I can't believe you have never been out throwing Frisbees into galvanized chain link baskets."

"I guess going to the beach all those times with my friends throwing the flat circular object back and forth paid off Joe."

"If you're feeling up to it Julie, we can walk a short distance to the lake where we can cast our lines from the sandy shoreline."

"You bet I'm up for it buster, I am here to get out and have a great time!"

At their spot they grabbed two fishing poles, a red plastic tackle box and a white bucket just in case they happen to catch any fish.

They also brought along two green fold out camping chairs to sit on. It is almost a mile hike on a narrow dirt trail to get to the big lake known as Diamond Head.

A cool comforting breeze is gently blowing on the bank as the two set their things down under the shade of a big maple tree with vibrant colored red leaves.

Julie unhooks the leash from Muffy's collar sitting the small dog loose to roam about. The thirsty terrier makes its way to the water's edge lapping up a drink of cool water.

"She's got the right idea; did you happen to bring any beverages with us?" Julie inquires gazing over at the bearded man.

"I did but it won't be ice cold anymore." Joe explains taking the two bottles of Gatorade from the tackle box.

Upon baiting up their small metal hooks, the pair cast out into the green fresh water in front of them. Simultaneously they sit down peering out in the distance across the large body of water.

Toward the middle of the lake are a few motorboats cruising on the relatively calm water most of them are pulling a skier or people on inner tubes.

A little over an hour lapsed by when Julie catches the first fish that put up a heck of a fight. It is a good size catfish that has long black snake like fillers on the side of its mouth.

Joe manages to catch one two inches shorter than his camping partner's, "I know what we are going to have for dinner tonight."

"Big guy you are the one who has the honor of gutting these beauties because you are probably better at it than I happen to be."

"Not a problem I live for stuff like that."

Shortly before five that afternoon, the couple decided to call it quits when they begin feeling hungry. Once again Joe and Julie gathered up their belongings then hoofed it back to their camp site.

Subsequent to making it back, O'Connell prepares the two fish while Guthrie grabs one bundle of wood from the back of the truck.

She uses a hatchet to chop up some kindling prior to starting a fire in the shallow pit that is surrounded round river rocks.

When the fire is going well the long haired man flips over the heavy steel grate. He places a black iron skillet on it to cook the catfish in it, then shakes a little garlic salt followed by a dash of cilantro on them.

In no time at all the pleasant fragrance of the cooking fish fills the summer air. "I don't think I ever had fish cooked over an open fire before." Guthrie comments.

"You've been seriously missing out then girl!" Joe teases her after flipping each fish.

On the second day the couple walked around the trails by the lake then went for a swim in the nice cool green water that refreshed them from the heat.

That night in the dusk of the tent, each of them are lying on their sides staring into each other's eyes talking about the day's events.

O'Connell makes his move first by leaning in close putting lips on hers. They begin to make out passionately the soft blown up air mattress that is under their two sleeping bags.

In no time at all the two of them are completely naked pressed tight against each other's bodies. Similar to the first time they had sex the big hairy man starts getting physically rough once again.

Though it is a pleasurable sensation to Julie, she doesn't like the way he man handles her while he makes love. It almost feels as if she is a victim of an abusive person.

Following the uncomfortable session of intercourse, the two put their undergarments on and went to bed without saying a single word.

Most of the night, the red head laid on her back looking up at the nylon ceiling wondering what she is doing with the man lying next to her. Even though Julie likes Joe as a person, she doesn't feel right about any kind of romantic link between the two of them.

Chapter 6

Three months later, the wishy washy minded young woman is still steadily dating Mark and Joe. Julie is coming to a point in her life where she wants to settle on being with one person on a continuous basis. Her confused thinking is creating added stress at work making reporting difficult.

Saturday November twenty around eleven seventeen in the morning, Julie is still in her pajamas watching TV with a cup of coffee thinking about her boyfriends.

"Maybe my best friend will help me decide which one I should be with in my life?" She thinks to herself prior to going to the phone dialing up her buddy.

"Hey Tammy, are you busy today?"

"Not really why?"

"I'm confused about something and need someone's insight to help me with my troublesome indecision."

"Ok let's go to my restaurant, there's a private spot where we can talk Julie."

"Thank you so much, I'll be there in a jiff."

Pulling open the entrance door, Guthrie sees her friend behind the cash register next to one her long time waitresses that is a little overweight.

When Tammy notices Julie she promptly ambulates toward her direction with a pleasant smile on her face. "There is a perfect spot in the lounge where we could talk privately. Are you hungry?"

"I'm starving I haven't ate yet."

"George's famous grilled chicken sandwich you love so much is what you need right now with fries and salad. It's on the house today I will go tell him right now. Go have a seat in the bar area there is nobody in there right now."

"Thanks Tammy! If it's not too much trouble could I have glass of lemon lime soda?"

"Of course you can, you're going to need wash that food down!" Nelson says just prior to going to the kitchen while her walks to the lounge in the rear of the building.

As usual the twenty one and over area is dimly lit with music down low playing over an expensive Japanese audio stereo system.

Various beer and whisky advertisements decorate the walls in the good size room that serves a large amount of regular patrons throughout the week.

The distraught red head sits in the far corner of the room at a booth facing the bar that is a short span away. A large transparent glass of pop and ice is placed on the surface in front of her.

"Your food will be here in around fifteen minutes or so." Tammy says previous to sitting down across the table. "What is bothering you?"

"As you know I've been dating two guys fairly regularly as of lately."

"From what you've told me over the phone and when we've met at the gym they sound like a great couple of men."

"Believe me Mark and Joe are so cool to have around but my heart tells me to choose one of them! For the life of me I can't decide which one I should be with!"

"You have a very bleak look on your face, is your situation causing you to great anguish?"

Before answering the question Mindy brings the food then places the plate in front of the hungry news caster. "Thank you!" Julie says prior to taking a big bite from the sandwich followed by taking another sip from the straw.

"Mentally I feel messed up; I'm constantly wondering if I'm doing the right thing. Sometimes I lie awake thinking not able to sleep most of the night. Other times I don't eat because I have a deep sensation of anxiety."

"To me you're experiencing a bout of depression. I can't tell you which guy to choose but I can put you in contact with a clinic my husband's friend used after his divorce here in Santa Monica."

Swiftly Nelson jots down the information on a small notebook pad she removed from her upper breast pocket of her brown shirt.

A sincere look in the restaurant owner's brown eyes as she presents the piece of paper to her close friend that was ripped free from the little spiral notepad.

Bright Meadow Depression clinic at 3521 Halford Blvd, Santa Monica, 403-555-4718 is written in black ink on the blue lined paper.

Julie looks up from reading, "This is the one that is right next to the homeless shelter. I've passed by it many times over the years."

"Please let me know how it goes after you have a session depression councilor!"

"I will certainly do that Tammy!"

After finishing her lunch, Julie thanks her friend for the information and for the delicious hot meal before going back to her apartment.

Around six thirty that evening, Mark walks up behind Joe who is sitting at the bar on one of the round stools with a glass mug of cold beer before him.

The "Lime Light" tavern is mildly busy having a few customers playing video poker while a young man and woman are playing darts on the other side of the room.

"Excuse me; may I have a few words with you Joe?" Hansen nervously requests.

Slowly the long haired bushy bearded man turns his head glancing at a clean cut gentleman who is wearing slacks and white button up dress shirt.

"Is there something I could do for you partner?" Joe asks in a deep voice.

"I need to talk to you about Julie for a few minutes."

"Sure we can talk about her but you have to play me a game of pool because I'm a little bored right now!"

"It's a deal!"

Faded denim jeans along with a newer looking Harley shirt is the tall welder's attire as he grabs the billiard balls from the bartender then strolls to a middle pool table.

Joe breaks first with a hard forward thrust sending the triangle form of colorful round balls scattering across the green felt surface. Two strips fall into separate pockets from the loud crashing break.

"I know that we have been seeing the same woman, I've been content with the arrangement thus far Joe. For me the time has come for Julie to pick either you or myself to be in a relationship."

"That same thought has entered my brain also Mark, so what kind of game plan are we going to go with?"

"How I believe we should handle it is the two of us step of our dating skills. Each of us do our very best to win her over in the weeks to come then give her an ultimatum about picking one of us." The lawyer declared then shot one of his solids balls into the side pocket.

In thought, O'Connell rubs his black chin hairs with the thick fingers of his right hand while leaning on the vertical pool stick.

"Slim you might be onto to something with your little scheme. You're on, may the best man win, but let's finish this pool game first."

"Who knows which one of us she'll pick big guy."

"Heck, maybe she won't pick either of our sorry butts to have around her!"

"It is definitely a possibility that could happen!" Both men begin to laugh after the ironic comments they shared in between taking shots.

Monday morning at ten, the distraught red head gets the piece of paper out of her black leather purse. She promptly dials up the counseling number with her heart beating fast from being a little nervous.

After a few audible rings, Bright Meadow Depression Clinic Audrey Ward speaking, how may I help you?"

"My name is Julie Guthrie I got this number from a friend to help me with my depressed thinking."

The woman on the other end of the phone asked the news broadcaster a few questions to determine if she qualifies for a research medicine.

Upon answering the almost fifteen minute inquiries into the phone receiver, Nurse Ward tells her she is a candidate that may come in for the next step.

"Friday this week as of now has several openings Ms. Guthrie. Is that day going to work for you?"

"Yes Friday is fine, but I need a morning appointment because I work in the afternoon."

"Is nine thirty going to be alright?"

"That time will be very doable for me."

"I will put you down on the calendar. Do you have any questions for me?"

"No not at this time."

"See you Friday Ms. Guthrie."

Friday morning a little past nine, the new patient leaves Muffy with her elderly couple before going to the depression clinic on Halford Blvd.

At nine fifteen, Julie parks her four door compact car across the street from the tan's stucco clinic that has black iron bars over the windows.

A short distance to the right of "Bright Meadow's" entrance door is three scroungy looking individuals wearing wore out dirty clothes.

Two of them are smoking cigarettes while the one who isn't is talking loud and belligerent as she appears to be visibly intoxicated.

Julie quickly walks past the homeless people fearfully not looking their direction as she made her way to the clinic's glass front door.

Inside the lobby, the uneasy client views to rows of metal legged thin cushioned chairs, there are a few glass tables with an assortment of magazines on them.

Perambulating toward the counter is two white females with their hair put in buns talking to each other. They are both wearing dark purple scrubs for their uniform.

The one sitting down looks up at the red head, "May I help you miss?"

"My name is Julie Guthrie; I have an appointment today at ten."

The slender Caucasian woman glances down at the appointment book that is resting on the white counter top surface in front of her.

After locating her name the polite receptionist made her way over to the filing cabinet fetching out many sheets of white paper.

"Please have a seat over there to fill out the required forms; someone will be coming to get you shortly."

Grabbing the white pieces of paper on the clipboard, a hopeful news caster sits down reading each of the typed forms before signing or writing her information down.

Just following completing all the necessary paperwork, an average height chubby African American nurse comes out of a solid dark stained wood door.

She has the attractive TV personality follow her into the other room for the determining examination. Sharing pleasant conversation, the two woman casually stroll a short way down a narrow hallway to the examining room.

Entering the small room with a bar weigh scale, tall grey padded examination table next to it is a small digital heart rate monitor machine.

On the far left side of the room is a tan counter with a clipboard on the surface. There is a small stainless steel sink built in to the short counter top.

There are nature pictures on the walls of beautiful scenic places that one might take a vacation at to make the patients feel more comfortable.

Julie turns facing the dark skinned lady flashing a nervous smile not knowing what to say next. "Sorry about my bad manners, my name is Rhonda Ward." She says just prior to getting the clipboard.

"Nice to meet you, forgive me for being so jittery. I've never done this kind of thing before."

"We'll try to make this as pain free as possible Ms. Guthrie. Please step on the scale; I'll need to jot down your current weight."

Right foot first the clinic's newest patient climbs up the white protective paper covered table. A crinkling sound can be heard as she sits her back side onto the padded surface.

Ward checks her patients' blood pressure and temperature then writes down on the piece of paper attached to the clipboard.

The nurse sits down on a chair in front of Julie, "I will need to ask a few questions before you do the blood and urine tests here in a little bit."

Most of the inquiry is about her medical history along with how she has been feeling recently about things in her life and if she is allergic to any medication.

Guthrie is taken to another area to have her blood drawn as well as a urine analysis. A tall thin Hispanic male nurse with thin black mustache drew three tubes of the pale skin young woman's dark red fluid.

The Mexican man with the strong accent gives Julie a small transparent plastic cup with a screw on lid then has her use the provided restroom.

Subsequent to the final test of the heart rate monitor, Guthrie was led by a short white male physician who had to readjust his horn rimmed glasses with thick lenses back on the bridge of his nose.

"Hello Julie, my name is Dr. Roberts; let's go to my office for the final in your journey today with us."

He takes her to his decent size office to attempt to pinpoint the distraught woman exact problem with even further questioning.

Walking through the open door, she peers across the street to where her dark green Toyota is parked by way of a large glass window.

"Please have a seat Ms. Guthrie!" The doctor says as he goes around his desk in the far corner of the room.

Black hands of the large round clock mounted on the wall say that is nearly one thirty in the afternoon already. "Darn it, I've already been here for four hours now!" Julie thinks to herself as sits on the dark brown leather chair in front of Robert's big wooden desk.

Perusing around the room, the news caster sees several plaques on the wall of the physician's achievements while he asked her several questions.

Close to an hour goes by of the clean cut man asking question after question writing down what the bothered female responded by saying. He even had a pen recorder picking up their shared dialogue.

"Thank you for your time today, I will be contacting next week to let you know of the finding results."

"I look forward to hearing from you; hopefully something can be done to ease my mind." Julie tells him then shakes his hand.

The two politely say good bye to one another, followed by Guthrie exiting the room while the doctor sits down back at behind his desk.

Leaving the front entrance of the building, the bright rays of the sun hits the fair skin beauty right in her green eyes causing her to squint. She travels home in a matter of minutes through the lightly congested traffic that is moving smoothly.

Under the warm water of the shower that feels so good against her bare skin the Californian native begins gazing down at her belly.

She starts to notice that it is sticking out a little more than normal then rubs her soapy washcloth over the surface of her tiny belly button.

"Crap I'm starting to gain a bit of weight to my gut! I seriously need to get myself back to the gym routine more often than I have lately with Tammy! It wouldn't hurt me eat foods with a lot less calories involved as well." She softly says under breath while continuing to wash her petite body.

Chapter 7

Coming days consist of Mark buying gold jewelry for his item of affection as well as expensive name brand perfume. He speaks more from the heart when he sees her about how much he loves being with the news caster.

Joe shows his charm by having a dozen red roses from the local flower shop along with a sugary sweet card that he wrote a message telling his feelings towards her.

Though the two men's behavior is currently out of character, the pretty Californian girl doesn't notice. Julie's mind is totally preoccupied with the change in her body along with wondering what the clinical results could be.

Friday early afternoon, the red head with her hair pulled back in a ponytail from just coming back from the "Better Fit" gym is turning the key in her doorknob.

Suddenly the phone starts to ring as she pushes through the apartment's front entrance. She briskly rushes in then throws the small duffle bag from her shoulder onto the living room couch.

Guthrie makes it to the telephone by the fourth ring, "Hello, this is Julie speaking!" She informs breathing a little hard from hurrying.

"This is Dr. Roberts with the "Bright Meadow Depression" clinic. I don't know if you are aware of this but you're pregnant. We cannot prescribe any of our available depression medicine to women who are expecting a child."

"I am what doctor!"

"Your lab tests showed you are currently pregnant Ms. Guthrie. I know a good obstetrician that my wife and I used years ago."

"Could I please have their name and number to make an appointment to deal with my present situation."

"Dr. Thomas Cartwright, according to my notes in front of me his phone is 555-4528. His practice is located at 2719 SE Howard Drive here in town. From the condition you are in may create mood swings from hormones becoming somewhat off balance in your body."

"Thank you very much for all of your assistance Dr. Roberts."

"You're very welcome Julie, I wish you the very best. Sorry we couldn't have been more help here at the clinic!"

Julie hangs up the phone sits down at her small dining room table and begins sobbing from the shocking news. Her thoughts on the matter instantaneously became worrisome on how she is going to handle it.

A troubled young woman ponders which of the two men in her life could actually be the father as well as how she is going break the surprise to them.

Obsessing on whether she is even pregnant at all, the compulsion to find out has her drive to the grocery store picking up several different brands of pregnancy test.

Glass of water after glass of water is drank in preparation to pee on the white applicator test sticks. By the third glass Julie has the urge urinate for what she deems necessary.

One by one the tests displayed in their own way that the TV personality is in the state of pregnancy. White test stick in her left hand having a panic attack dials up Tammy Nelson to release the emotions.

"I'm going to have a baby! My god what in the world am I going to do! You managed to be with Brian for fourteen years with having happen! Why did it happen to me?" Julie is speaking loud and fast into her telephone receiver.

"Calm down! How do you know for sure that you are even pregnant at all?"

"The depression doctor called me up saying that the lab they sent my blood and urine samples to determined that I have a small life growing in me. Not to mention I took three EPT tests in a row over the toilet! Each of the darn things presented positive results to me being pregnant!"

"Please breathe easy and try to relax, I will help you in any way that I can! Are you planning on keeping the baby?"

"There's no way that I could ever bring myself to having an abortion. It is my mistake and I need to do what I believe is the right thing."

"That was what I was hoping you would say, have you told Mark and Joe yet of your present day condition?"

"No I haven't. I plan on sitting each of them down at different times calmly explaining the situation. When the time is right I will be insisting that they take a paternity test because there is no way I could stand not knowing!"

"Give me the low down of how your fellas take the life changing news. We'll have to take our work outs a bit easier during your pregnancy phase."

"Thanks for listening to me, I feel better now."

"That's what friends are for Julie!"

"I'll let you go; I need to take care of a few things in my hectic existence."

The coming week that ends the month of November is a very uneasy time for the green eyed beauty as she has the task of the breaking announcements of the baby.

Monday morning the on edge broadcaster goes to her boss's office telling Sherece of her pregnancy as she sits behind her desk sipping a cup of hot cup coffee.

"Young lady please don't be concerned about losing your job here at the station. You are not the first news reporter to be having a baby in front of the camera."

"Can we keep it between you and me for a little while? I need to tell people close to me in my personal life before the community finds out."

"The only persons I'll tell are channel two producer and director who happen to be above me in status here. I will personally tell them to keep the information under their hats for right now."

For three days straight when Julie's mind wasn't focused on performing her job she intently pondered about who was to be the first man to be told. Where along with how came in to her pain staking thinking on the important subject.

Thursday afternoon around five thirty, Guthrie convinces O'Connell to meet her at Malley's Pub because she has something to tell him.

Cold ice tea is sipped into the lips of the anxious red heading as she watches the big bearded man stroll her way carrying a full pint of micro brewed lager.

He sits down across the small brown table from Julie, takes a large gulp from the glass before sitting down on the dark stained surface.

"What's up not having your usual glass of white wine?"

"My doctor doesn't advise me to consume any alcohol in my present condition."

"Is there something wrong with you?" He asks displaying a puzzled look on his rugged face.

"Joe the reason why I called up to meet me here is because I am nearly four months pregnant."

A speechless man sits staring momentarily into her bright green eyes totally surprised by the announcement. "I thought you were just getting a little fat this whole time." The husky welder says before taking another gulp of beer.

"For a while I was under the impression that I was just becoming heavy from my bad diet."

"Julie are you saying I am the father of your child or something?"

"As of now I'm not sure who the daddy is for the baby growing inside of me. It is between you and Mark who did the deed"

"If you want me to do a paternity test, I will be more than happy to oblige in doing it. What you've just told me has thrown me for a loop, I need some time to let this marinate in my confused brain! I will call you in a couple of days, please make arrangements for me to be checked out." A troubled appearing guy quickly finishes the cold amber liquid in his thick triangular shape pint glass then stands up walking away without another word.

All the distressed woman could do was silently sit, watching her big beau exit from the local pub with a sick feeling in the pit of her stomach. She has never been treated so coldly by a member of the opposite sex.

Not seeing Joe's face scruffy face again crossed the pregnant young lady's mind for a brief moment previous to calming down again.

"Mark had better be more understanding than that rough guy that took the news a little hard!" Ms. Guthrie thought to herself as she sat alone finishing the tall glass of ice tea.

Heart in hand Julie slowly perambulates up Mark's red brick paved walkway toward his tans arched entry beveled glass double doors.

An emotional expecting mother called Hansen the night before arranging to meet him that Friday afternoon to talk over something she has to say.

White flashy smile displayed by the attorney at law as the well-crafted door is opened for the nervous lady he has been seeing for a while now.

"You're here early; it's only four forty six. Come on in, I have some leftover chicken cacciatori that I baked last night." He said while shutting front door behind his guest wearing the casual shin length loose fitting lavender dress.

"No, I'm not hungry but I would like a glass of some kind of fruit juice if you have any left."

"Right now all I have is pink lemonade in my fridge, if that's ok with you!"

"Perfectly fine, I'm feeling a bit parched right now!"

"What a pretty dress you have on, it is a lot less form fitting that I viewed you before."

"Found this old thing in my closet and just decided to where it again."

"Anyway, go have a sit wherever you wish and I'll come find you with your cold drink."

Julie decides to go out making herself comfortable on one of the cushioned chairs that are set out on the pressured treated wood patio deck.

"Hopefully I can choose the words to perhaps notify Mark gentler than I did the other day!" She thinks to herself while enjoying the view from the comfortable spot.

Handing her the glass then sits next to her close on the right side, "Is there something pertinent that you need to discuss with me?"

Uptight sensation causes Guthrie to take a drink of the cold pink liquid prior to answering the direct question, "This is isn't easy for me to say?"

"Whatever it is that you have to tell me, I'm sure a rational guy such as myself will totally understand." A soft spoken Hansen explains.

"Here goes nothing, I'm pregnant and I don't know if it's your baby or Joe's!"

The tan good looking lawyer stands up without a verbal response going back inside his lavish home through the sliding glass door.

Instantly tears flow from her green eyes from feeling rejected by the man she deeply cares for. "Men are such bastards! I am so through with them! They are all the same every last one of them! If you tell them you're having a baby they leave!" The distraught woman said to herself.

Minutes later Mark comes strolling up with a small boutique of flowers, a greeting card and a small brown teddy bear with a tag hanging off its left ear.

He hands the gifts to the red head with a surprise look on her face then promptly sits back down in the same chair. "I thought for sure were freaking out about what I told you. What is the deal with the presents?"

"On the contrary I'm not bothered at all about the announcement here this evening. As far as the bear and the card, they were going to be a gift for my brother's wife a couple of years but she lost the baby."

"These are such lovely flowers Mark!" She reads the card that says, "Congratulations!"

"I bought these earlier today to give to you to just show affection, but they certainly go well with the news of the child you are carrying."

"Joe has offered to take a paternity test when the time comes. What if the baby turns out to be his?"

"You can still keep the gifts that I gave you today!" They both start lightly laughing together. Julie wipes the tears from her eyes as she chuckles.

"Seriously Mark! What if the baby is not yours?"

"Basically for me it comes down to which of us you want to be with in a serious relationship!" His sincere blue eyes seem to look right through her as he speaks from the heart.

"Every inch of my inner being tells me that you are my soul mate! You are the man I want to be with for the rest of my life!"

"If it turns out that the baby is his, I will raise your child as if it were biologically mine giving the he or she all of my love and affection that I can!"

Like the two of them were reading each other's mind they stand from their seats simultaneously bracing one another tightly.

The pair begins expressing how much they love each other over and over in a happy tearful moment as light rain begins to shower down.

Passionately Mark and Julie kiss for a moment not paying attention to anything else before making their way inside the spacious home with her gifts.

Chapter 8

Brightly the sun shines through Julie's apartment window when Joe unexpectedly called her up around nine in the morning. "Sorry if I was a little rude the other day but the baby was the last straw in our multi dating circle that we have goin on together!

"Looking back at the shocking low down I threw in your face I can see now how a person might react that way. What are your thoughts about if my child turns out to be also yours as well?"

"For me living with a woman and raising a small child has never interested me. If the baby turns out to be mine, I will be more than happy to pay child support but I do not want to be in its life! My next door neighbor Maria and me have gotten more serious lately from seeing a lot more of each other."

"Mark has agreed to be in the baby's life whether it turns out to be his or not. We are now in a monogamous relationship wanting to raise the child together. So if it turns out to be yours can he adopt the boy or girl gaining legal custody?"

"Absolutely of course, what you're asking is a gigantic weight off my shoulders! Just let me know down the road when you want to take the test."

"I'll certainty do that Joe. Thank you, I will keep you informed."

"See ya Julie!"

After hanging up the phone, the expecting mother stands without taking a single step quietly saying out loud, "Please let that big lug not be the father if you're listening up in heaven dear God!"

Weeks go by before the stubborn minded news reporter calls up her parents in Idaho that are running their own hotel business off of a lake. She hasn't talked to either one of them since they left over a year earlier.

Following a pleasant conversation with her father he hands the receiver to his caring wife. "Hello dear, how are you doing?"

"I'm fine mom. I want to apologize for the fight we had before you left."

"Oh that was water over the bridge sweetheart, don't you worry about that. How is that news reporting job going for you?"

"Very well thank you! The biggest reason I called was to tell you and dad that I'm going to have a baby."

"About time, your father and I were beginning to think we were never going to become a pair of grandparents! Dear I hope it is as welcomed news to you as it is for us!"

"At first no, but the notion definitely grew on me. I am really looking forward now to become a mother."

"You bring that grandchild of ours here to spend some time with us shortly after it is born! Don't make me and your dad come looking for you. We will have a special room waiting here for the arrival of you two."

"Mom I promise I will make arrangements to do that after the birth happens. I'll let you go now; I will call you in a couple of weeks."

Julie's long dialogue with her folks gave the California girl a little more peace of mind by opening the door once again with the two important people.

In the passing months, Tammy as well Mark takes turns accompanying Guthrie to regular prenatal care appointments with her physician.

A baby shower is held at Nelson's house where many of the broadcaster's co-workers along with old friends she grew up with attended.

Cute baby gifts were unwrapped by the mother to be as many took pictures to capture the happy memory. Lots of tasty pastries are consumed by the cheerful party attendants.

On a quiet evening at Julie's apartment, her handsome boyfriend gets down on one knee front of as she sits upon the couch.

"Honey you are very special to me, I never thought I would want to spend the rest of my life with just one woman. What I'm trying to say is, Julie will you please take my hand in marriage?" Mark asks holding up a tiny box with the lid flipped open displaying a shiny diamond ring.

"Yes, of course I will handsome!" Her suitor gets off his knee then sits down beside the blushing bride to be.

"Now you ask me silly, once I'm five months along with a belly that is bulging out. We better arrange the wedding ceremony soon before my stomach won't fit into one of those fancy white gowns."

On a cloudy over casted Saturday morning, Mark and his friend Steven pull up in Julie's parking lot. The broadcaster's boyfriend is behind the steering wheel of a bright red moving van that he rented from a nearby business.

Trailing close behind the soon to be groom is his older brother Carl accompanied with Brian Nelson in a full-size Chevy pickup to help with the moving.

Julie's belongings will be taken over to her boyfriend's house where she will be living now with her Boston terrier Muffy.

Sunday afternoon the last box of the pregnant woman's belongings is unpacked from the cardboard boxes. She now has more room to hang up her beautiful wardrobe in the much larger walk in closet in the master bedroom.

Off and on in the passing days, the young couple writes out invitations for their guests to come to Carl Hansen's fifteen acre property for the ceremony.

June sixth is a mildly warm Saturday, when friends and family begin parking one by one on the long wide paved driveway of Mark's older brother.

It is a little before two in the afternoon when people began sitting down on rows of white wood folding chairs in the large grassy area behind the host's home.

Lovely lady guests are dressed in long vibrant colored dresses while the men are wearing designer suits and ties for the momentous occasion.

Soft instrumental music is coming through two speakers on the rear corners of the seating arrangement. Mark walks down in the middle aisle to the awaiting pastor wearing a black tuxedo with shiny black winged tipped shoes.

He goes to his older brother who is already standing up front close to where the bald man of God wearing wire rimmed glasses is holding his bible.

Organ music to the tune of "Here comes the bride" begins to be pumped through the speakers causing everybody to look back behind them.

A little curly hair blonde girl wearing a pink dress is throwing flower peddles from a small wicker basket she has grasped in her tiny right hand in front of her.

Behind the girl is the captivating bride who is escorted by her father who made it from Idaho with his wife the day before. Julie is wearing light pink wedding dress with a matching color lacy veil on her head.

She gracefully strides on the narrow red carpet under the warm Southern Californian sunshine. Upon telling the preacher that he gives the bride away, Wendell Guthrie makes his way back to his wife Sherri who sits looking on.

Groom and bride stand close face to face saying their sincere vows to express their devotion to one another. They added some of their own words to the customary verbal agreement.

A very happy young woman stares at the attractive bronze face of her soon to be husband as the minister reads the necessary portions to make it legitimate.

Minutes later the middle aged preacher says the words everyone is waiting to hear, "I now pronounce you husband and wife you may kiss the bride!"

Everyone stands up joyfully cheering as the newlyweds lock lips in a loving embrace to seal the deal. Mic in left hand, Carl informs that the reception is being held in the large enclosed tent down the hill a short span away.

Casually the guests make their way strolling in the direction they were just instructed the event was to be, while the newlyweds are driven there in a golf cart.

It is a fun filled get together after the wedding ceremony with plenty of food as well as beverages. Small time band, "Winged Destiny" is hired to play various styles of popular modern music.

Men, women and even a handful of kids dance as the four musicians perform on the small oval stage. Out of rhythm folks have a great time moving about on the soft grassy surface below their feet.

Later that evening, a long black limousine takes the bride and groom to a honeymoon suite at a tall beachfront hotel in Marina Del Ray.

For two wonderful days Julie and Mark enjoy the warm sandy beach as well as hospitable room service that the pricey establishment provides.

Powerful waves break on the huge rocks below as the content Mrs. Hansen looks down at the Pacific Ocean from her hotel room balcony with a cup of hot coffee.

Mark is sound asleep on the queen size bed as she stands barefooted wearing a red cotton nightgown outside of the sliding glass door.

Cool westward wind blows through her shoulder length hair as the fair skin woman is alone with her thoughts. "It took a while to come but I finally got married! He is definitely the right man for me to tie the knot with!"

Epilogue

Just over three months later, Julie Hansen gives birth to a seven pound five ounce baby girl that the couple named Margie Tabitha Hansen. The beautiful blessing is born at the Santa Monica Hospital, friends and family come to spend time with the newborn.

Three days following the birth on a Thursday, Joe lives up to his word by taking a paternity test. Mark chooses to take one himself a day after O'Connell.

Even though it is only a handful of day to find out the results, Julie has the sensation of being on pins and needles as time seems to have stopped.

A new mother has trouble falling asleep at night from the uncertainty of who the biological father actually is of her beloved Tabitha.

The successful attorney doesn't display any worry about the possible findings because he sees that the child has the same shaped nose as his. He has never mentioned the insight of the discovery to the pretty wife, Hansen savors every moment with the tiny little girl.

On a Wednesday morning, Julie is doing the dishes while the baby is sleeping when the phone rings. She dries off her soaking wet hand to answer the phone in the other room.

"Hello, is Mrs. Hansen home?" A female voice on the other end of the line inquired.

"This is her speaking! May I help you?"

"I'm Nurse Allison; I have both of the submitted DNA samples results for your recent paternity test. Would you like me to tell you today over the telephone or mail them to you?"

"Please tell me now, it means a lot to me to find out!"

"Our lab determined a 99.99% that Mark Hansen is the biological father to Tabitha."

Heart beating fast from the excitement of the call, Julie dials up her husband at his law office telling him the good news that he is officially her child's daddy.

A chuckling lawyer tells the hyper sounding woman that he had a hunch the adorable infant was his creation but didn't want to boast prematurely.

At noon Mrs. Hansen calls up Joe on his cell phone catching the welder on his lunch break to tell him the paternity news to ease the burley man's mind.

In a positive tone her ex-boyfriend thanks her kindly for calling him on the subject. He takes the time to congratulate her on having a baby as well as being recently married.

His deep upbeat voice helps add closer to everything that happened between the two of them many months previously in her life.

Julie and Mark have a boy a year later named Marty then called it quits on having any more children. Between raising her two kids Mrs. Hansen steadily continue to work as a television broadcaster along with occasional field reporting for channel two news.

In the years to come attorney Mark Hansen becomes a circuit court Judge for the city of Santa Monica and is able to spend more time with his family.

Joe dates his next door neighbor Maria for quite a while before the two of them sell their homes after her kids moved out.

They buy a house in the country where the big bearded welder lives with his loving girlfriend, dogs and various livestock that the pair raises.

As O'Connell would have it he and his long time sweetheart would never walk down the aisle together to get married. Both of them stay faithful one another for rest of their lives.

.